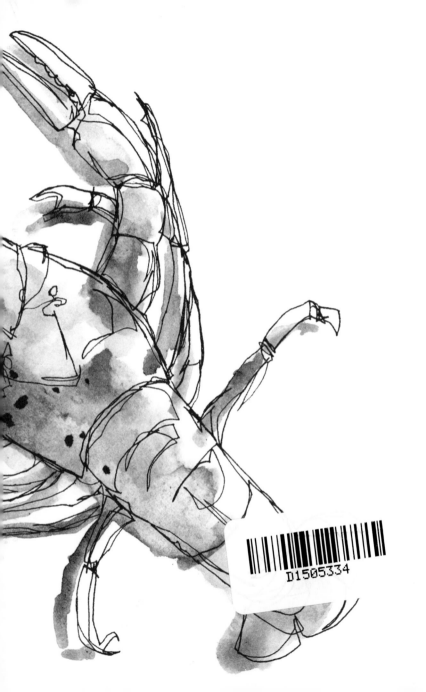

SPIT FEATHERS

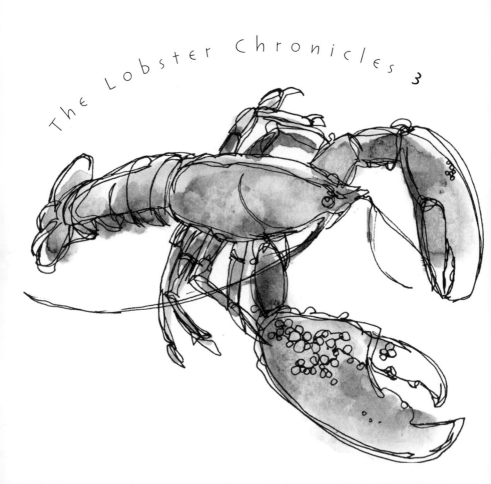

The Lobster Chronicles 3

SPIT FEATHERS

Jessica Scott Kerrin

Illustrations by
Shelagh Armstrong

Kids Can Press

To my parents, Bud and Mary — J.S.K.

Kids Can Press acknowledges the financial support of the Government of Ontario,
through the Ontario Media Development Corporation's Ontario Book Initiative; the
Ontario Arts Council; the Canada Council for the Arts; and the Government of Canada,
through the CBF, for our publishing activity.

Published in Canada by	Published in the U.S. by
Kids Can Press Ltd.	Kids Can Press Ltd.
25 Dockside Drive	2250 Military Road
Toronto, ON M5A 0B5	Tonawanda, NY 14150

www.kidscanpress.com

Edited by Sheila Barry
Designed by Marie Bartholomew
Illustrations by Shelagh Armstrong

This book is smyth sewn casebound.

Manufactured in Shen Zhen, Guang Dong, P.R. China, in 2/2013 by Printplus Limited

CM 13 0 9 8 7 6 5 4 3 2 1

Library and Archives Canada Cataloguing in Publication

Kerrin, Jessica Scott
      Spit feathers / written by Jessica Scott Kerrin ; illustrations by Shelagh Armstrong.

(The lobster chronicles)

ISBN 978-1-55453-708-2

      I. Armstrong, Shelagh, 1961– II. Title. III. Series: Kerrin, Jessica Scott.
Lobster chronicles.

PS8621.E77S65 2013   jC813'.6   C2012-904395-8

Kids Can Press is a ʦOrus™ Entertainment company

Contents

Burial

The trees in the birch grove swished overhead as Ferguson Beaver and two classmates peered into the box. Inside, a dead warbler rested its head on a pillow of tissue. Ferguson closed the lid and lowered the box into the tidy hole that he had just dug.

"A moment of silence, please," Ferguson said, his hands clasped respectfully in front of him.

Georgia and Deckland nodded in solemn agreement and clasped their hands as well.

But there was no silence. Lower Narrow Spit was awash with the *putta-putta* sounds of lobster boats returning home for the day, along with shrieks and laughter from the elementary school playground beside their grove of trees.

"Get off, Norris! It's my turn!" someone hollered in the distance.

The funeral party turned to see what the fuss was about. A younger boy named Allen stood shaking his fist at their classmate Norris. Norris was soaring above Allen's head on the playground swings.

"In a minute!" Norris shot back.

Norris.

Ferguson did not like him one little bit.

For one thing, Norris was a cheater. Ferguson had caught him that very afternoon trying to copy Ferguson's answers during their spelling test.

Norris also poked fun at Ferguson's clothes, which he said made Ferguson look like an old man. Ferguson smoothed the front of his checkered sweater vest and wondered why that was such a crime.

And then there was the matter of dodgeball, Norris's favorite sport. No matter how many times their teacher, Ms. Penfield, warned the class to aim the dodgeball *below* the shoulders, Norris always fired at the head. It was infuriating.

Ferguson knew, as did everyone in Lower Narrow Spit, that Norris could get away with all kinds of bad behavior because his dad, Edward Fowler, was the owner of the town's only lobster cannery. It was called Lucky Catch, and the cannery's logo — a cartoon lobster rowing a dory with its giant claws, tail flipped up as if to say "Look at me!" — was plastered about the community as a smug reminder.

It was even stamped on the box now serving as the dead warbler's coffin.

Fifty-eight one thousand, fifty-nine one thousand, sixty, Ferguson counted in his head. He spoke again at the one-minute mark.

"And now, the eulogy."

He reached into his back pocket and consulted his notepad, which he was never without. He cleared his throat.

"No one can say why our feathered friend flew into the classroom window."

"Maybe it was attracted to Ms. Penfield's cacti plant collection," Georgia offered, a bit too jovially for Ferguson's liking. "One of them even has a brand-new orange bloom."

Ferguson stared at her until she gulped in apology.

"No one can say why," Ferguson repeated, even more soberly. "But the world is sadder for having one less singer to join tomorrow's dawn chorus."

Ferguson paused for dramatic effect. He was pleased with his choice of the phrase "dawn chorus." He looked up, expecting to see both Deckland and Georgia deeply contemplating his words, perhaps even shedding a tear or two.

Instead, Georgia whispered something to Deckland, and Deckland checked his watch.

Ferguson frowned. No wonder animal burials fell to him. Even Graeme, a classmate who loved science and made sure that the school pets were fed correct diets, never directed funerals. Once something died, so did Graeme's interest.

Defeated, Ferguson signaled to Deckland to cover the box with the mound of dirt beside the gravesite. Deckland smoothed over the top with the shovel, then Georgia laid some dandelions and forget-me-nots that she had picked to mark the spot.

As a final touch, Ferguson inserted a small white cross made out of Popsicle sticks to serve as the headstone. He had written "Bird" along with the day's date on the cross in beautiful penmanship.

"I'm telling!" Allen howled from afar, killing the mood.

Both Deckland and Georgia fidgeted, but Ferguson was determined not to budge.

"Perhaps some music to conclude our ceremony," he suggested. He did not put it as a question.

"Okay," Deckland said, tugging at his shirt, "but just one song. I'm supposed to be the playground monitor today, so I need to see what's up with Allen."

"And I'm supposed to go with my dad this afternoon to place Tasty Foods' order at the cannery in time for the lobster festival," said Georgia, who often helped out at her family's minimart.

"A bird," Ferguson said, "has died. How terribly inconvenient for you both."

Georgia gave a long sigh through her nose. Deckland grumbled as he pulled out his harmonica. He played "We Shall Overcome," but not without a few errors in his haste.

As soon as the final note was played, Georgia and Deckland made a dash from the grove without so much as a backward glance.

Ferguson lingered behind. He surveyed the faded crosses that poked up this way and that, marking all the memorable funeral services he had conducted: Hamster, Garden Snake, Goldfish, Tree Frog, Salamander, Turtle, Goldfish, Goldfish, Bird. Then he sat down on a nearby moss-covered boulder to contemplate the view of the harbor across from their school.

"The best cemeteries have ocean views," Ferguson's grandfather had once told him. "You make sure that's where I end up. I want the view." And he had jabbed Ferguson in the chest for punctuation.

Everything Ferguson knew about funeral services he had learned from his grandfather and his grandfather's retired fishing buddies at Sunset Manor, the seniors' residence in Lower Narrow

Spit. His grandfather had moved there more than a year ago, and Ferguson had been attending funerals ever since.

But one service stood out among all the rest. McDermit's.

McDermit had been his grandfather's friendly rival, a lobster fisherman whom his grandfather had known since they were boys. When McDermit died, his family donated many items that he had made to Lower Narrow Spit's community museum.

"A remarkable legacy," Ferguson's grandfather observed whenever Ferguson took him to the museum so that he could marvel at McDermit's exhibit. "His handiwork was mighty fine!"

But that admiration soon gave way to worrying thoughts. Ferguson's grandfather had become obsessed about leaving something of his own behind when his time came.

"What's my legacy?" he asked whenever

Ferguson came to visit, which was every day after school.

More than anything, Ferguson wished he had an answer.

The wind swirled through the grove of birches again, this time tossing some of last year's brittle leaves into the air, like tiny fluttering kites. One of them rose well above Ferguson's head.

There it hovered, just long enough to give Ferguson a terrific idea that might put an end to his grandfather's search. But before he could tell his grandfather, Ferguson had a stop to make along the way.

Bat Kite

Ferguson marched steadily home along Main Street, barely noticing the usual sights: Graeme's house with his old beagle, Fetch, sprawled on the porch; Deckland's house with its giant whale bone on display in the front garden; Georgia's house with its plastic lawn chairs inside a screened-in bug tent to keep the blackflies off; and Allen's house with its yard covered in folk-art whirligigs.

As Ferguson rounded the bend, he could hear his own deafening household long before he could see it. Ferguson came from a large family of sisters, eight in total. And they were all named after flowers: Iris, Violet, Poppy, Petunia, Jasmine, Daisy, Lily and Rose.

No wonder he spent so much time at Sunset Manor.

Ferguson slowed down with deliberate care, in an attempt not to attract any attention from his sisters. He picked his way across his yard's minefield of topsy-turvy toys, around the abandoned tetherball pole and past an incomplete set of scattered lawn darts. An expert at moving under the radar, he eased through the back door, making sure not to creak the hinges. His mom had an after-school rule: no one (no one!) was allowed inside until suppertime.

Ferguson stopped in his tracks to listen. From the distant whirring sounds, he guessed that his mom was in her sewing room working on her latest order. She was a seamstress and had her own business called Forever and For Always. She specialized in wedding gowns.

The whirring continued. The coast was clear.

Ferguson tiptoed past the kitchen sink stacked with drying dishes and into the dining room, where the table was crowded with homework projects in various states of completion. He wedged his arm behind the sideboard and pulled out his kite. It was bat-shaped and not very girly, but that had *not* proved to be the deterrent he had hoped for when he had built it in Deckland's garage.

Hence the hiding spot.

Ferguson slung the kite over his shoulder and headed out the door with a brilliant plan on how to solve his grandfather's legacy dilemma. All Ferguson had to do was turn his grandfather into Sunset Manor's best kite flyer, ever!

Ferguson was barely outside when he heard his name.

It was Iris calling as she got off her bike.

"Just getting back from the cannery?" he asked.

Iris, still in high school, had a part-time job there.

She nodded, then began to untie some empty boxes stamped with the cartoon lobster from her basket.

"Where do you want them?" she asked.

Iris kept Ferguson supplied with coffins of all sizes, just in case.

"The porch for now, I guess," he replied.

"I saw your classmate at the cannery," Iris said as she unloaded the boxes.

"Who? Norris?" Ferguson asked. It was an easy guess because Norris regularly dropped by his dad's office after school.

"He sure thinks he owns the place," she continued. "He barely stopped in the hall to say hello to me."

"That'd be Norris," Ferguson said, shifting his bat kite to the other shoulder. "He thinks he owns the school as well."

"How so?" Iris asked, taking off her helmet and smoothing her hair.

"Just before Ms. Penfield left to have her baby, she assigned Norris, of all people, to take care of her cacti plant collection."

"I remember Ms. Penfield's prized collection," Iris said fondly. "She always entered a cactus or two at the lobster festival's plant fair. Think she'll enter again this year?"

"Probably. One of them is in bloom."

"Well, I won't get to see it. With the way the boiler keeps breaking down at the cannery, everyone is expected to work overtime to meet all the extra orders," Iris grumbled. "I'll probably miss the entire festival."

"Georgia told me about placing an order for Tasty Foods today," Ferguson said, recalling with annoyance her hasty departure from the warbler's funeral.

But annoyance with Georgia turned to a

smidgen of sympathy for his sister. The annual lobster festival was a very big deal in Lower Narrow Spit, and not to be missed. In a little over a week, hundreds would descend to participate in the festivities.

There would be the Princess Mermaid and King Neptune Pageant, which would be presented on a temporary stage in the parking lot of the cannery. Graeme's little sister, Lynnette, had won last year. She still liked to prance around in her tiara and pretend she was married to Allen, who had been appointed King Neptune but had flung his crown off the government wharf as soon as Lynnette was not looking.

There would be the contest for building lobster traps, as well as lobster boat races in which the captains had to follow an obstacle course set up in the bay. That always drew huge crowds, although Ferguson's grandfather said that the crowds had been even bigger back when he and McDermit took turns winning for twenty-two years in a row.

There would be the lobster parade on Main Street, weaving through town and marching right past Ferguson's house. Deckland had already spilled the beans about the float his family's hardware store was going to enter: a giant constructed lobster waving carpenter tools.

There would be the lobster chowder contest, held at the community museum, which Georgia planned to win with her very own creation. The postmaster's wife had won that contest the year before with her combination of traditional ingredients based on a family recipe handed down for generations.

There would also be the wildly popular arts and handicrafts fair. Last year's most creative entry was a bedside table lamp made from stacked-up lobster cans by Heimlich Fester, a Sunset Manor resident.

And as always, the festival would culminate in the main event: the lobster supper and auction. This took place in the old dance hall next to the town's small cluster of commercial buildings: the curling rink, the bank, the drugstore, the post office, the hardware store, the minimart, the community museum and the diner that sold famous Chinese take-out with special lobster sauce.

Ferguson had already offered to bring his grandfather and a few buddies from Sunset Manor to the lobster supper and auction. Which reminded him: he was supposed to be on his way to pitch an idea for his grandfather's legacy. He turned to leave and called over his shoulder.

"I'm off to visit Granddad."

"You're bringing your kite?" Iris asked. "You don't expect him to fly that thing, do you?"

"I'll be back in time for supper," Ferguson replied, an expert at ignoring endless sisterly advice.

Ferguson was still walking along Main Street when he heard whoops and laughter down at the government wharf. He paused to see what the ruckus was about and could make out a large group of fishermen in their rubber overalls standing beside the lobster boat owned by Graeme's dad.

Then he spotted Norris leaving the cannery, which stood next to the wharf. Norris scooted across the parking lot in a great hurry and headed straight up Main Street toward Graeme's house.

That weasel, thought Ferguson, forgetting his kite mission. He charged toward Norris, determined to confront him about his latest bout of cheating, which Ferguson would have done earlier if the unfortunate warbler had not flown into the window right after the spelling test.

"Norris!" Ferguson shouted as soon as he was within earshot.

Giant Lobster

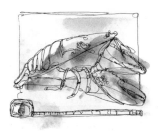

Norris froze. He quickly glanced to the left and the right, obviously looking for bushes or garbage bins to hide behind.

There were none. Norris had no choice but to hold his ground.

"What's up?" he asked innocently, his braces flashing in the late afternoon sun as he picked at his scabby elbow.

Ferguson strode to within a fraction of where Norris stood.

"You know what's up!" Ferguson accused.

"You're one gigantic cheater! I could just spit feathers!"

Spitting feathers had been McDermit's favorite expression. It was one of the many sayings from Sunset Manor that he had recorded in his notepad.

"Try not to go overboard," Norris said, but he furiously jingled the coins in his pocket, which he always did whenever he was about to start a fight. "Who cares about spelling, anyway? As far as I can tell, the rules are just made up. It's all pretend, if you ask me."

How typical of Norris to dismiss a subject that mattered to Ferguson!

"Words are not *pretend*," Ferguson challenged. "In fact, they're more real than people, if you think about it."

Norris stood baffled. He stopped jingling.

"What?" he asked, his jaw dropping.

"Words are more real than people," Ferguson repeated.

Norris stared blankly at Ferguson.

"People die, but words go on and on and on. They're *eternal*," Ferguson explained. "That makes them more real than you or me."

Ferguson smugly hitched the kite higher on his shoulder. McDermit's words came to life whenever Ferguson said them, so Ferguson knew what he was talking about.

"You're creeping me out," Norris finally admitted.

He rubbed his scratched-up arms, which Ferguson guessed was the result of watering Ms. Penfield's overcrowded collection of prickly cacti.

Serves him right, thought Ferguson.

"What's with the bat kite?" Norris asked.

Oops, thought Ferguson. He had gotten sidetracked once again.

"I'm going to fly it with my granddad. He lives at Sunset Manor."

"Sunset Manor? Where all the old fishermen live?"

"Senior citizens," Ferguson corrected. He did not like Norris's condescending tone.

"Must be a dull place," Norris said. The coin jingling returned. "I hear they just sit around making gawd-awful crafts for the lobster festival. Graeme won a lamp made of lobster cans last year. It was hideous."

"They do more than crafts!" Ferguson argued. "There's ping-pong and cards and lawn bowling and museum outings and" — he lifted the bat — "kite flying."

Norris did not look impressed. But then his face lit up.

"Say," Norris said. "My dad bought our land at Marshy Hope from an old fisherman named McDermit. I'm pretty sure he moved to Sunset Manor."

Ferguson knew all about Marshy Hope.

McDermit had built his fish shed there and spent his off-season months mending nets, painting buoys and shooting the breeze with younger fishermen seeking his advice.

"He's not at Sunset Manor anymore," Ferguson said, his anger turning to sorrow. "He died a year ago. My granddad still misses him."

Norris looked as though he was going to say something else insensitive, but then thought better of it.

"Have you seen the giant lobster?" he asked instead.

It was Ferguson's turn to stare at Norris as if he had two heads.

"What giant lobster?" Ferguson asked dubiously.

"Graeme's dad caught it," Norris explained.

"McDermit caught a giant lobster back in the day," Ferguson recalled. "He once showed me a newspaper article about it in his scrapbook."

"The one just caught is still at the wharf, if you want to go see it," Norris suggested. Norris was always up on the latest gossip because of his constant eavesdropping.

Ferguson glanced back at the crowd of fishermen, then licked his pointer finger and held it up to test the wind. It was starting to cool down for the evening. Good thing he was wearing a sweater vest.

"I can't. The wind's going to die soon," he said reluctantly, hoisting the kite higher over his shoulder, but he still lingered.

A giant lobster was a rare event in Lower Narrow Spit. Ferguson hated to miss it. Norris seemed to read his mind.

"They'll be moving the lobster to the community museum for now," Norris said. "You could go ask your grandfather if he wants to check it out later this week."

"That's not a bad idea," Ferguson admitted.

Norris's surprisingly considerate suggestion distracted him from the whole cheating episode, which, of course, he would remember later that evening as he tossed and fumed in bed.

Ferguson continued down Main Street toward Sunset Manor, bat kite in tow. When he arrived at the seniors' residence, he slipped into the back of the recreation room. Today was the poetry workshop, and the seniors were sitting at tables that formed a U-shape to face the podium. Ferguson surveyed the room, looking for his grandfather, while Tupper Hastings, one of the residents, stood at the front reading his poem out loud.

Tupper Hastings was comparing growing old to fruit cocktail with all the good parts picked out. He was somewhat deaf, so he read extra loudly. It made the poem sound comical, which was probably not his intention, judging by his serious expression.

Ferguson spotted his grandfather wedged between two other seniors, both of whom had nodded off. Ferguson waved to try to catch his eye, but his grandfather was furiously writing and paid no attention to Ferguson or to Tupper Hastings.

Ferguson skirted along the wall, past the hanging quilts, the BINGO chart and the watercolor paintings that mostly featured flowers in a vase, except for one, his favorite, which was a lobster fisherman on a boat lowering a trap.

"Psssssst," Ferguson said.

His grandfather jerked his head up, then smiled when he saw Ferguson. He quickly gathered his things, and they made their way out of the room.

"Thanks for the narrow escape," Ferguson's grandfather announced, the door to the recreation room not yet closed. "I hate poetry."

"Really? Then what were you writing about?"

Ferguson asked, noting that half the class was staring after them, while Tupper Hastings valiantly pressed on.

"I was revising my obituary."

Ferguson's grandfather had been working on his obituary ever since he moved to Sunset Manor, claiming that it was the only way he was going to have the last word. He had even prepaid the town's newspaper for a quarter-page section, and he had already selected a photo to be included in the article. It featured him wearing a giant pumpkin costume at Halloween. The only thing left to write was the part about what legacy he would leave behind.

"Let me see," Ferguson said.

Ferguson read the draft, and to no surprise, the legacy part remained blank.

"What do you have there?" Ferguson's grandfather asked.

"I was thinking that maybe you could learn to fly this," Ferguson offered, holding up the bat kite.

"And become Sunset Manor's champion kite flyer!" his grandfather deduced. "That'd be a great addition to my obituary! Let's give it a try!"

Seventeen Pajamas

Ferguson and his grandfather headed outside to the manicured lawn with the pleasant flowerbeds, but by then, the wind had completely died.

"Keep the kite," Ferguson suggested. "We can try again another day."

Plans postponed, they turned a couple of chairs around to face the window of the recreation room, then sat down.

"Look who's reading now," Ferguson's grandfather said. "Laverne Bridge. That's one lady who's got her curlers wound too tight."

Ferguson studied the elderly woman at the podium. She was wearing a flower-patterned pantsuit and a giant sparkling brooch. She was gesturing grandly, and the two men who had nodded off earlier now sat up wide awake.

"Graeme's dad caught a giant lobster today," Ferguson remarked as they watched. He knew that his grandfather loved to hear all news from the government wharf.

"You don't say," Ferguson's grandfather replied, turning his full attention to his grandson. "Is it as big as the one McDermit caught? *That* was a real corker!"

"I don't know," Ferguson said. "But it's going to be moved to the community museum. Maybe we should check it out next week."

Ferguson's grandfather nodded, but then the next poetry reader distracted him once again.

"Oh, look. It's Heimlich Fester's turn. If he

writes one more thing about the time he was abducted by aliens, I'm going to have a stroke."

"Heimlich Fester is senile," Ferguson reminded him.

"No, he's not. He's just pretending to be," Ferguson's grandfather said, arms crossed.

"So what about a trip to the museum?" Ferguson persisted. He loved the museum and its fishing exhibits because of the stories his grandfather told during their visits.

"Sure, sure," his grandfather said. "I hear they put more of McDermit's handiwork up on display."

Ferguson and his grandfather sat in silence as Heimlich Fester read his poem, then sat down.

"Uh-oh. Buddy Clark," his grandfather observed, brow furrowed, as another speaker headed to the podium.

"Isn't he the new one from out west?" Ferguson asked.

"What gave it away?" his grandfather replied. "Those ridiculous cowboy boots he prances around in, messing up the linoleum with a trail of ugly black scuff marks wherever he goes?"

"I like those boots," Ferguson said.

"Swears he's going to be buried in them," Ferguson's grandfather grumbled.

"Proper thing," Ferguson said.

"Umph," his grandfather replied.

Ferguson turned to his grandfather. People said they looked identical: same height, same large ears, same taste in clothes. When Ferguson saw his grandfather, he saw his own future with, he hoped, just as many of his own stories to tell someday.

"Who should we take with us to see the giant lobster?" Ferguson asked.

"Hastings, I guess," his grandfather said. "His poem wasn't all that bad."

Ferguson's stomach rumbled, and he dutifully got up from his chair.

"I better get home for supper."

Ferguson knew that if he did not get to the table on time to lay claim to his share of the meal, there would be nothing left but the vegetables. He bent to kiss his grandfather's stubbly cheek.

The next morning during math class, Ferguson was scratching out some calculations in his scribbler when he became aware of an evil presence over his left shoulder. It was Norris leaning well beyond his own desk, attempting to peer at Ferguson's work.

Ferguson shot him a dirty look, then hunkered down and protectively covered his answers.

Norris pulled a face, then returned to his own scribbler. It had lots of blanks, and there was hardly any class time left to fill them. He muttered something that Ferguson was sure was not very flattering about sweater vests.

Ferguson sat back in his chair. He was sick of Norris, and it was not just the constant cheating or the wardrobe mocking or the vicious dodgeball attacks. His anger stemmed from way back when Norris had ruined Ferguson's very first big birthday party.

That was in grade one. Ferguson had invited the whole class, including Norris, who was too new to be treated with the suspicion that he now so richly deserved.

Ferguson's mom asked Ferguson what theme he would like his party to have, and he replied, "Horses!"

He had been thinking about cowboys and the wild, wild west.

His mom and sisters tried their best. They decorated the backyard with pink and purple ponies featuring long flowing manes and thick curly eyelashes. Some had braided tails with ribbons.

But even that was okay. After all, the party had been filled with games like Pin the Tail on the

Donkey and Simon Says; the smashing open of a piñata that looked like a cowboy hat; and no dodgeball despite Norris's nonstop whining to play.

Everyone ate a piece of the horseshoe-shaped cake from Tasty Foods, and then it was time for presents. A stack of them beckoned from the picnic table.

"Open mine first," Norris insisted.

Ferguson unwrapped Norris's package. It was a pair of plaid pajamas and a matching housecoat. His sisters ooohed and aaahed as they felt the plush fabric.

Ferguson looked at Norris, confused, and Norris merely shrugged.

He tossed aside the pajama set and opened his next gift.

It was also a pair of pajamas, but with fire trucks printed on them.

He opened his third gift: pajamas with a frog print.

His fourth gift: pajamas with dinosaurs.

His fifth: pajamas with skulls and crossbones. Sure, they were pirate pajamas, but still, they were pajamas!

In fact, every gift — *all seventeen* — was a pair of pajamas.

Ferguson burst into tears and fled inside to his room.

Later that week during art class, Norris made his confession. The two boys had been working on paperweights to give as presents for Father's Day, when Norris said, "I didn't pick your pajamas. My mom did. I knew that pajamas weren't a good gift, so I had to tell everyone else that you really liked pajamas. That way, my gift wouldn't look so bad."

Ferguson was stunned.

"Why did you want me to open yours first?"

"I knew you wouldn't like my pajamas, but I

also knew that you wouldn't like the seventeenth pair even more."

It was then that Ferguson knew Norris was diabolical.

Ferguson glared at the paperweight that Norris had been making, a water-filled clear plastic container that he sealed with a boat and a lighthouse on an island inside. It was a skillful attempt and quite beautiful.

When Norris was not looking, Ferguson sabotaged it. He made a tiny pinprick near the bottom, so tiny that the water would leak out unnoticed over time.

Ferguson had not thought about that ruined paperweight for years, but now he relished it on the walk home from school. His thoughts were interrupted when Iris pulled up beside him on her bike as he turned up the driveway.

"I didn't know Norris could spell. Looks like you have a rival," she teased, handing him a couple of empty boxes for his collection.

"Why would you say that?" Ferguson asked.

"Sixteen out of twenty is a pretty good score."

"How come you know his score?"

"His dad posted Norris's test on his office door at the cannery."

"That *cheater*!" Ferguson bellowed. And he followed up with a few of his grandfather's choice curse words — words that were even more colorful than spitting feathers.

Fish Shed

Sunset Manor was hopping with Friday evening activities when Ferguson arrived for his daily visit. The recreation room had been converted to a dance studio, and a young instructor was teaching a class called Tap Dance for Seniors. Ferguson poked his head into the room just as she started the music, some jazzy horn number from long ago.

The seniors, having formed three lines, tapped and clapped to the beat, except for Tupper Hastings in the back row, who appeared to be dancing to another tune only he could hear. He kept bumping into others or crushing their toes.

Ferguson's grandfather was not there, so Ferguson continued to the common room. It was teeming with elderly people talking over each other and the blaring televisions that no one seemed to be watching. Amid the din sat a group of card players, including Ferguson's grandfather.

Ferguson sidled over and had a look at his grandfather's hand, while his grandfather stared without blinking at Buddy Clark across the table. Buddy Clark adjusted his cowboy hat and narrowed his eyes, but said nothing. Ferguson could tell that the game was not going in his grandfather's favor. Buddy Clark had accumulated a huge pile of bottle caps in comparison to his grandfather's miserable half-dozen.

"I fold," Ferguson's grandfather announced, slapping his cards down on the table in disgust. He forced his chair back, angrily scraping the floor, then scooped up the bat kite, which had been leaning on the table beside him.

"Were you flying the kite?" Ferguson asked as they left the players.

"I was going to, but that trickster talked me into a card game instead," Ferguson's grandfather explained bitterly. "Let's give the kite a try now."

"There's no wind," Ferguson reported, recalling the dozen or so empty clotheslines that he had passed on his way to Sunset Manor. "How about a game of Scrabble instead?"

Ferguson's grandfather surveyed the room and smiled when he spotted Laverne Bridge and Heimlich Fester working on a puzzle.

"I'd love a game," he said eagerly. "Let's set up near the puzzle champions."

There was something in his tone that put Ferguson on high alert. His grandfather was definitely up to something.

Ferguson retrieved the Scrabble set from the shelves jammed with every boxed game imaginable. He set it up on a table beside the puzzle makers, and they each claimed a letter from the alphabet bag. Ferguson drew the letter E; his grandfather drew the letter K.

"You start," said Ferguson's grandfather, glancing quickly at the puzzle table, then choosing his first set of letters.

Ferguson studied the letters he had selected and rearranged them on his rack.

"F-O-G," he spelled out loud as he placed his word horizontally on the board. "That's fourteen points." He recorded his score in his notepad and picked up three new letters.

"Ha!" Ferguson's grandfather said extra loudly, causing the puzzle makers to look their way. "H-O-R-N. Foghorn," he announced as he laid his letters down, building on Ferguson's word. "Fifteen points."

Ferguson wrote down the score. He returned to his letters.

"B-O-A-T," he announced, building off the first letter O in "foghorn." "Six points."

He looked up at his grandfather, who was staring at the puzzle table and stifling a chuckle.

"What's going on?" Ferguson asked, drumming his fingers on the table.

"Nothing," his grandfather said innocently as he raised his bushy eyebrows. He straightened his face and studied his letters.

"L-I-F-E. Lifeboat," he announced, picking up replacement letters. "That's fourteen points."

Ferguson recorded his score.

"S-I-Z-E," he said, delighted to build off the letter I in "lifeboat" and to use the letter Z, which by itself was worth ten points. "That's thirteen total for me."

But his grandfather barely noticed. He was eavesdropping.

"There're too many blue pieces," Heimlich

Fester complained. "I'm telling you! The aliens are trying to mess with us."

"Stop that talk," Laverne Bridge said with a dismissive wave of her hand.

Heimlich Fester reached for the box with the picture of the puzzle on the cover.

"Don't show me the picture! That's cheating!" she scolded. "I'm an expert. I don't need the picture!"

She frowned as she tried to force a blue piece to fit with the others.

Ferguson's grandfather silently laughed, his chest heaving up and down.

"Your move," Ferguson said, finding nothing funny about the frustrations at the next table.

Ferguson's grandfather returned to the game at hand.

"C-A-P. Capsize," he stated. "Twenty points on a double word score."

Ferguson was getting trounced. He glumly

added forty points to his grandfather's total and expected to be teased.

Instead, his grandfather had returned to eavesdropping.

"You're being ridiculous," Laverne Bridge said with pencil-thin lips when Heimlich Fester got up with a fistful of blue pieces and stood by the window, staring up at the sky as if searching for a secret signal.

Ferguson's grandfather resumed his silent chortling.

"M-A-Y," Ferguson declared, laying his letters down and building on "capsize." "Eight points on a double word score for sixteen points!"

"D-A-Y," his grandfather said. "Mayday. Fifteen points."

Ferguson reviewed the scores. He was still losing badly. Foghorn. Lifeboat. Capsize. Mayday. This was a shipwreck of a game, and his grandfather was not even paying attention!

Laverne Bridge stopped pounding a piece into place and angrily reached for the box with the picture. Ferguson's grandfather burst out laughing.

"I mixed the puzzles!" his grandfather confessed, slapping his thigh. "I wondered how long it would take for an expert to figure it out!"

Ferguson knew that his grandfather loved practical jokes — whoopee cushions, an exploding can of springy snakes, sugar in the salt shaker — but lately, Laverne Bridge seemed to be the target of more than her fair share.

Laverne Bridge scowled as she stood. She wagged her knobby finger in their direction without a word before grabbing her walker and storming from the room. Ferguson's grandfather chuckled until she was all the way out the door.

Ferguson shook his head. He looked at the wall clock. Time for supper.

"You win," he announced, scraping the letters

off the board and into the alphabet bag. In his haste, one of the letters dropped to the floor. His grandfather scooped it up.

It was the letter X.

Instantly, Ferguson's grandfather quieted. He slipped the letter back into the alphabet bag, while Ferguson regretted ever suggesting the game.

The letter X had been skillfully carved by McDermit to replace a missing letter just months before he died. It was yet another reminder of the many creative projects that McDermit had left behind to be remembered by.

Ferguson grew quiet, too. He had to admit that his champion kite-flying idea was off to a very slow start. Perhaps he should look around home for another legacy in case the bat kite did not work out.

But where to search?

The attic? The basement? The garage?

Just a few months ago, Graeme had taken him into his dad's shed to choose an object that they could bring to school as part of their project on ocean trade routes. Inside were all kinds of curious items that Graeme's dad had hauled up in his nets and displayed on the shelves: old, round-bottomed bottles and fragments of china; anchors from pirate ships and a pewter galley spoon with chew marks; an old lead sounding and cannonballs from battles long ago. There was even an unusual fine-toothed comb made out of bone, which Graeme's dad was going to donate to the community museum.

Well, Ferguson's grandfather had a shed, too. Maybe Ferguson could search it for something of his grandfather's that would serve as a legacy.

He kissed his grandfather's sunken cheek. "See you tomorrow," he promised.

His grandfather nodded, then put away the game with shaky hands.

Wooden Floats

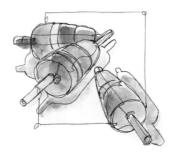

Ferguson strode past a peeling, upside-down dory on the way to his grandfather's fish shed, which was perched on stilts over the water behind Ferguson's house. The shed had taken on a rakish lean, and one of the windowpanes had blown in, but Ferguson could still make out the hand-painted sign that read "Lobsters 4 Sale." Above that sign, his grandfather had nailed a birdhouse that McDermit had made.

The birdhouse was occupied. Ferguson could hear tiny *cheep-cheeps* from within.

He pulled open the door and stood at the entrance. The shed remained chockablock with old and broken equipment that no one (no one!) was allowed to throw out: a grinding wheel, a battery charger, wire brushes, wooden crates, sounding weights, hand-line reels, tackle blocks, antique sled runners, dory paddles with leather-wrapped handles, rubber boots.

Ferguson examined this object and that. Because of the fishing stories he had recorded in his notepad, he could identify almost all of the spare boat parts that his grandfather had squirreled away. Ferguson did not stop until he came upon some handmade wooden floats painted in orange and blue, his grandfather's signature colors to mark his territory of lobster traps. They lay forgotten in the corner, probably untouched since the day his grandfather had sold his boat.

Bingo, Ferguson thought.

He grabbed an empty feedbag and piled

the floats into the sack. Then he hauled his treasure outside and closed the shed-door latch. Hoisting the feedbag over his shoulder, he lugged the floats to the community museum, which was located in an old train station that trains no longer visited.

"Hi, Deckland. Hi, Georgia," Ferguson said when he went inside and discovered his classmates standing beside a large fish tank holding an enormous lobster. "This must be the lobster Graeme's dad caught," he observed. "It's huge."

"Graeme's dad is going to auction it off at next weekend's lobster festival," Georgia said. "They'll use the money for a trip to Big Fish Aquarium."

The three paused to watch the magnificent catch, its antennae making slow swoops above its giant head. In the background, Ferguson could overhear the museum director talking on the phone in her office.

"It sounds like Ms. Carrington is speaking to a reporter about the lobster," said Ferguson.

The other two nodded, then returned their attention to the tank.

"Look at its crusher claw," Deckland said in awe. "I bet it could snap off a finger, just like that."

A number of residents at Sunset Manor were missing fingers, or parts of fingers, but that was mostly due to accidents with boat winches. Still, Ferguson was not about to stick his hand in the tank any time soon.

"What do you have there?" Georgia asked, spotting Ferguson's feedbag.

"Floats from my granddad's shed. He wants to leave a legacy, like his old friend McDermit. So I thought I'd help him out and see if I can donate these to the museum."

"I'll show you what my favorite object is," Georgia said.

She scooted across the room and stood in front of a plaque that was framed by rope.

Ferguson and Deckland joined her to study the plaque. It featured lobster claws that were stuck in place with plaster of paris.

"McDermit's wife made it," Georgia said.

"She used to work at the cannery," Ferguson recalled. "That was where she probably collected the claws."

"Until Norris's dad took charge and laid off some of the staff," Deckland added.

Everyone grew silent at the mention of Edward Fowler.

"Well, hello!" Ms. Carrington said, standing at her office door. "The giant lobster is attracting quite a crowd! You've just missed your classmate. Graeme's been coming by every day to feed it."

"Can I talk to you?" Ferguson asked, using his official business voice.

"Certainly," Ms. Carrington said, one eyebrow raised.

Ferguson hefted the feedbag into her office. He unloaded the wooden floats and arranged them in a line across her desk.

"I'd like to donate these," Ferguson said with a showy sweep of his hand. "As my grandfather's legacy."

Ms. Carrington fingered the floats and sighed.

"Oh, dear," she said hesitantly. "Maybe it would be better if you came with me."

She led him to the museum's storage room, formerly the place where the old train station kept luggage. Inside, stacked high, was a pile of wooden floats in every possible shape and color combination, donated by various fishing families of Lower Narrow Spit.

"I see," Ferguson said, shoulders slouching. "You already have too many."

"I'm afraid so," she answered. "But keep

looking. The museum is always on the hunt for unique items, like the plaque of lobster claws you were just admiring."

"Okay," Ferguson said without much hope, now that he knew his grandfather's shed contained nothing really special.

Ferguson dragged the wooden floats home. He sat on the deck of his grandfather's shed, listening to the *cheep-cheeps* and watching the salty fog roll in and turning everything a sodden gray.

Having completely lost his bearings, Ferguson decided to pay his mom a visit.

"No Food" read the cranky sign on her sewing-room door. Ferguson knocked softly. He dutifully waited until she opened the door. Just a crack. Even though he could only see a slice of her, the measuring tape dangling around her neck told him that she hoped the interruption would be short.

"Can I come in?" he asked.

"Let me see your hands," she demanded.

Ferguson held them out, tops first, then palms up.

His mom clucked her tongue at the oily grime, evidence of his time spent in the fish shed.

"I'll go wash," he said sheepishly.

Ferguson plodded down the hallway to the nearest bathroom. He dug through a pile of hairbrushes, combs and barrettes to unearth the soap dish. He sudsed up, rinsed, then wiped his hands on the front of his sweater vest.

Back down the hall he trudged, passing a few secret hiding places for his most prized possessions: his compass behind the radiator; his bird whistle on top of a framed painting of a lighthouse; and his fid kit that his grandfather had given him to splice rope, which was tucked under the cushion of the hall chair where no one ever bothered to sit. Outside, screams and laughter from his sisters wafted through the window beside the chair.

Ferguson knocked again. When his mom opened the door, he automatically held out his hands.

"Good," she said upon thorough inspection, swinging the door just wide enough to let him through. "Remember to take off your shoes."

Ferguson kicked them off and went inside, a fish out of water.

Cafeteria

As usual, the sewing room was awash with white:
white walls; white bolts of fabric neatly stacked
on white shelves; a rack of white dresses; a white
ironing board; a white mannequin posing in
a half-pinned dress, which was white; a white
cutting table; a white sewing machine with white
thread; a white-framed three-way mirror; and a
bulletin board tacked with photographs of the
brides of Lower Narrow Spit. They were all
wearing white.

The room also came with strictly enforced
rules, which Ferguson had dutifully memorized

over the years. He quickly reviewed them in his head. No touching. No sitting. No borrowing of scissors to cut wire for catapults.

"What are you working on?" he asked.

His mom held up an elf-sized white satin cape.

"For the crowning of this year's Princess Mermaid at the lobster festival pageant," she explained. "I've still got to sew all these on," she continued, pointing to a pile of tiny stuffed lobster claws made out of the same white satin.

Ferguson admired the intricate sewing that this project demanded. It reminded him of how his mom had taken the seventeen pairs of pajamas he had gotten for his birthday and cut them into miniature squares that she sewed into an elaborately patterned quilt for his bed.

He still loved that quilt.

"Very elegant," Ferguson said, choosing a word that he knew his mom would like and that his sisters used a lot.

"So, what did you want to see me about?" his mom asked, hanging the cape on the rack with the rest of the gowns, then flipping through the white satin hangers to evenly space her work.

"I'm worried about Granddad," Ferguson said, shoving his hands in his pockets, the best way to adhere to rule number one.

"What do you mean?" she asked, turning to give him her full attention.

"He's getting into trouble with the other seniors. And he's worried about what to leave as his legacy. It's all he thinks about."

Ferguson's mom walked over to the window and looked at the old fish shed.

"I remember hearing him every morning getting up early and heading out to his lobster boat while I lay cozy in my bed," she recalled fondly. "He was quite a fisherman in his day. McDermit, too. And this bay was full of lobsters. Good-sized ones."

"I guess there're still some big ones out there. Graeme's dad just caught a corker."

"Really? I remember McDermit's giant lobster. Your grandfather took me to see it on the wharf the day McDermit brought it in. That story even made the newspaper."

"I saw the article," Ferguson said. "McDermit pasted it in his scrapbook."

"What will Graeme's dad do with the giant lobster he caught?" Ferguson's mom asked.

"He's keeping it at the community museum until he can auction it off at the lobster festival. I'm going to take Granddad and Mr. Hastings to see it."

She turned to the pattern she was cutting on her table and picked up her pair of scissors. She began to snip precisely, letting the extra bits fall to the whitewashed floor.

"Your grandfather just needs time," she said. "He'll figure out his legacy soon enough." She looked up at Ferguson and her voice softened. "Trust me."

Her words wrapped around him like the comforting quilt on his bed. He headed out the door to retrieve his abandoned shoes.

On Saturday afternoon, after polishing off a peanut butter and banana sandwich, Ferguson dropped by Sunset Manor, just as the lunch crowd was in full swing at the cafeteria.

"Everything's so geezly bland," his grandfather grumbled, mixing his peas with his mashed turnip, having already gobbled up his meatloaf.

When the vegetables were gone, he soaked up the remaining gravy from his plate with a piece of bread and scarfed that down, too.

"Have you eaten?" he asked Ferguson as he chewed.

Ferguson nodded.

"Well, have my milk," his grandfather offered, as he always did.

Ferguson gulped it down. Sunset Manor's milk was the real thing, not the hateful powdered stuff his mom stirred up and served at home, because no one (no one!) could keep up with the milk consumption of nine children.

Tupper Hastings, who sat at the table with them, was already on dessert. Today's choice was mint Jell-O, chocolate pudding or fruit salad. He had chosen fruit salad and was chasing the red cherries with his spoon.

Laverne Bridge, also at the table, watched the two with a look of mild disdain as she sipped her tea, her lavender-tinted gray hair catching a shaft of afternoon sun. She sported another giant dazzling brooch. It seemed to Ferguson that she had an endless supply.

"When did you and Mr. Hastings want to go to the community museum to check out the giant lobster?" Ferguson asked his grandfather.

"What giant lobster?" Laverne Bridge asked,

setting down her cup and making a big deal about looking to Ferguson for an answer, not his grandfather.

"Graeme is one of my classmates, and his dad caught a giant lobster in one of his traps."

"Didn't McDermit catch a giant lobster in his day?" Laverne Bridge asked, now turning to Ferguson's grandfather with a mocking edge to her voice.

Ferguson's grandfather took a moment to answer, because he was scooping out the last of his chocolate pudding with gusto.

"Yes, he did. Made the papers, too," Ferguson's grandfather confirmed, dropping his spoon into his empty bowl with a clatter.

"I read that article," Ferguson added. "There was a photograph of him standing beside the giant lobster on the government wharf."

"Do you remember my boat in the picture?" Ferguson's grandfather asked proudly.

"You bet," Ferguson said. "McDermit pointed out *Fog Burner* to me. He pointed out Mr. Hastings's boat, too."

"That's right," Ferguson's grandfather said. "Hastings's boat, *Crack of Dawn*, had followed me in that day. We were both at the wharf when McDermit tied up."

"McDermit," Laverne Bridge said wistfully with a faraway look. "I sure do miss him."

"We *all* miss him," Ferguson's grandfather said with gruffness in his voice.

There was a heavy pause before he turned sharply to Laverne Bridge.

"He had a wife, you know."

"I know that," she snapped. "But he was a widower when he arrived at Sunset Manor!"

Ferguson thought back to McDermit's funeral and how he had been buried next to the ocean-view gravesite of his wife, Audrey. Her headstone featured a garland of tulips and trumpets.

McDermit's had an anchor flanked by thistles.

Ferguson's grandfather muttered something under his breath. Ferguson could not make it out exactly, but he knew that it was probably not very nice.

"Don't you dare judge me!" Laverne Bridge barked. "Here you are, with a grandson coming to visit you every day, and who do I have? No one! Just a large collection of jewelry from relatives who never have the time to drop by!"

She abandoned her tea and plowed out the door with her walker.

Tupper Hastings stopped pursuing his red cherries and looked up.

"What?" he said, adjusting his hearing aid.

"Nothing," Ferguson's grandfather replied, shoving his empty food tray away.

Ferguson wondered if another chat with his mom was in order.

Life Ring

Buddy Clark and Heimlich Fester set down their lunch trays and joined the table, unaware of the quarrel that had taken place.

"Hi, Ferguson," they said simultaneously as they unfolded their napkins.

"Ferguson was just asking me about an outing to the community museum," Ferguson's grandfather said, more himself again.

"Well, you can't go this afternoon," Buddy Clark said. "It's your turn to call BINGO, remember?"

"And tomorrow afternoon is crafts. You promised you'd help this time," Heimlich Fester said.

"What about Monday?" Ferguson suggested.

"Won't work. I'm in charge of the ping-pong tournament on Monday. Besides, Hastings has an ear appointment that day."

"Tuesday?" Ferguson asked.

"Hastings won't go out two days in a row," Ferguson's grandfather said.

"Wednesday, then?" Ferguson asked.

"Sure, sure. But let's make it over lunchtime," Ferguson's grandfather suggested. "Wednesday's fish cakes are gawd-awful. We'll check out the giant lobster, then have a look at McDermit's new stuff on display."

His voice trailed off at the mention of McDermit's name.

Ferguson was certain that his grandfather's sadness might be lessened if his legacy dilemma could be solved. So even though Ferguson understood why Ms. Carrington had rejected his attempt to donate his grandfather's floats to the museum, it was still frustrating. If only there was another place to display the floats where they would be appreciated.

He smiled. There *was* another place. Sunset Manor!

"Hey, Granddad," Ferguson said. "What if you organized an exhibit of everyone's fishing gear in the common room. I could help you set it up in time for the lobster festival. I'm sure it would be a hit."

Ferguson's grandfather rubbed his stubbly chin, pondering Ferguson's homemade museum idea.

"I like it," he finally declared. "We could call it the Know the Ropes Show."

Ferguson knew the phrase well. Knowing the ropes meant having a great deal of experience on a boat. It was one of the sayings he had recorded in his notepad.

"That's a great name," Buddy Clark said. "And I've got stuff to put in."

"You don't know squat about boats,"
Ferguson's grandfather argued.

"Well, I certainly know a thing or two about
rope!" said the retired cowboy, tucking his napkin
under his chin, Wild West style, instead of laying
it on his lap like the others. "In fact, I could give
some pretty fancy lassoing demonstrations. That's
always a crowd pleaser."

The two elderly men exchanged icy glares.
Ferguson weighed in so as to avoid another
explosive cafeteria scene.

"Granddad, what would *you* like to put into
the show?" he asked, thinking that his grandfather
might come up with something even better than
the floats Ferguson had found in the fish shed.

"Don't know. Seems all I've got left are a few
old tales about the times I was the captain of
Fog Burner."

Ferguson loved those stories. His grandfather,
when he lived with Ferguson's family, used

to tuck Ferguson into bed every night with a fishing story: spectacular storms and hitting unmarked rocks, getting lost in the fog with a broken engine or, most commonly, the big fish that got away. Ferguson had written down the best ones.

"You want stories? I've got stories," Buddy Clark said, snapping his suspenders against his chest. "And Heimlich here has some pretty fantastic ones, too, if you like science fiction."

Both he and Ferguson's grandfather chuckled, while Heimlich Fester unfolded a piece of tinfoil from his pocket and carefully laid it under his plate before beginning his meal.

"What about *Fog Burner*'s life ring?" Ferguson's grandfather suggested. "Do you still have that hanging in your room?"

The life ring had been hanging above Ferguson's bed ever since his grandfather moved to Sunset Manor.

"You bet," Ferguson said, nodding eagerly, because a life ring would be easier to transport than the feedbag of floats that Ferguson had hefted earlier.

"Bring it in so I can have a look. It might need a touch of paint before the show."

"Will do," Ferguson said, standing up to leave.

Ferguson had a good feeling about the Know the Ropes Show. If it was the giant success that he thought it could be, then maybe the show would become an annual event at Sunset Manor, in honor of his grandfather.

And his grandfather could finally put his legacy search to rest.

"You're not staying for BINGO?" Heimlich Fester asked, looking up at Ferguson.

Heimlich Fester insisted that space aliens were trying to communicate to him via BINGO letters and numbers. He also felt that he was very close to cracking their code.

"Another time," Ferguson said kindly, and he waved good-bye to the people at the table.

The next morning, while Ferguson was still tucked underneath his pajama quilt, someone burst into his room.

"Ms. Penfield had her baby!"

Ferguson rolled over and lifted his head off the pillow to see which of his sisters had ignored his "No Girls Allowed" door sign this time.

"A girl!" Iris added.

"Oh, boy," Ferguson muttered, rolling back to face the wall. "Just what we need more of around here."

Then Iris did what all his older sisters did whenever they could pin him down: she licked her finger and stuck it in his ear.

Ferguson howled, but to no avail.

Later that morning, Ferguson unhooked the life ring from his wall and returned to Sunset Manor, but not before running into Norris on Main Street.

"What's with the life ring?" Norris asked without so much as a hello.

Ferguson held up the old canvas-covered memento for better viewing. The name *Fog Burner* had been painted on by hand.

"This was my granddad's," Ferguson explained. "He hung it in my bedroom when he retired."

"Your grandfather owned a boat named *Fog Burner*?" Norris asked.

"Nothing gets past you," Ferguson said dryly.

"Where are you going with it?" Norris asked.

"My granddad wants to display it at the Know the Ropes Show."

"What's the Know the Ropes Show?" Norris asked, picking at his scabby elbow.

"We're going to organize Sunset Manor's own museum exhibit, as part of the lobster festival. Everyone will put something in, mostly old fishing gear and boat stuff, and then sit around and talk about lost trophies."

"Lost trophies?" Norris repeated.

"You know. A million fishing stories that all end in 'the one that got away,'" Ferguson explained.

Norris's eyes flickered, which was a sure sign that he was about to lower a trap.

"Can I come?" he asked.

"No," Ferguson said without any hesitation.

"Why not?" Norris asked. He started to jingle the coins in his pocket.

"My birthday party is why not," Ferguson said. "You can't be trusted at events."

Norris heaved a sigh.

"Oh, come on! That was a long time ago. And anyway, I have something to put in the show. Something made by your grandfather's old fishing buddy, which makes my object extra special."

"Who?" Ferguson asked suspiciously.

"McDermit," Norris said, rocking on his heels.

"McDermit," Ferguson repeated, eyes widening.

But then he remembered how Norris's family had bought the land and fish shed at Marshy Hope from McDermit. That meant Norris was probably telling the truth.

"So I'm in?" Norris asked, his braces glinting in the sun.

It was Ferguson's turn to heave a sigh.

"I suppose," Ferguson said, knowing that his grandfather would love to see what Norris had of McDermit's. "Come by Friday after school. That's when we'll be finished setting up."

He continued on his way to Sunset Manor, the life ring somehow feeling as heavy as a feedbag of wooden floats now that Norris had become involved.

Paddle

When Ferguson arrived at the grounds of
the seniors' residence toting the life ring, he
discovered his grandfather dragging the bat kite
behind him, with Tupper Hastings cheering him
on from the sidelines.

"Have you gotten it to fly, yet?" Ferguson
asked.

"Sort of," his grandfather said as he shuffled
past Ferguson, yanking the kite across the grass.
"But not really," he added. He turned to Tupper
Hastings and held out the ball of string attached
to the kite. "Your turn."

Tupper Hastings took the kite, then proceeded in a more or less straight line across the lawn at an even slower pace than Ferguson's grandfather. The kite obediently skated along the ground behind him.

"Faster!" Ferguson's grandfather called out.

"What?" Tupper Hastings replied, slowing down even more.

Ferguson licked his finger and held it up in the air.

"There's not enough wind," he observed.

"You're probably right," Ferguson's grandfather said. He retrieved the hapless kite from Tupper Hastings, who looked very glad to hand it over.

Ferguson proudly held up the life ring.

"What do you think?"

Ferguson's grandfather took a long time to reply. When he did, he sounded all choky.

"I think I should never have given up my fishing boat."

His lower lip trembled.

Tupper Hastings thumped his back fondly, then crept away to join some other seniors sitting on a circle of lawn chairs.

"But you still have all the stories," Ferguson said. "Let's go inside and see about painting this for the Know the Ropes Show."

They walked across the expansive lawn and into the main common room area. At the sight of the ping-pong table, Ferguson's grandfather perked up.

"Have a look at the tournament sign-up sheet," his grandfather said.

A list of names had been posted on the wall near the table.

Ferguson scanned the list of ping-pong partners who would be playing together. Beside his grandfather's name was the name of his would-be partner, Laverne Bridge.

Only, her name had been crossed out by angry red pen strokes.

"Why is your partner's name crossed out?" Ferguson asked.

"It is?" his grandfather replied, genuinely surprised.

He peered at the list.

"Humph," his grandfather said upon confirming the deletion.

"What happened?" Ferguson asked.

"A difference of opinion, I guess," his grandfather said, shrugging off the snub, but still wearing a small mischievous smile.

"I'll be your partner," Ferguson offered.

"Great! Bring your paddle tomorrow."

Ferguson signed his name above the scratched-out one. Then they headed to the recreation room, where the paint was kept.

The recreation room still sported last week's poems posted on the bulletin board inside. While his grandfather rummaged through the paint cupboard, Ferguson read some of them.

"Hey, here's one you wrote," Ferguson exclaimed, pointing to a poem written in his grandfather's handwriting. "'Hope Breathes' by Arthur Beaver."

"What's that now?" his grandfather said, jerking his head out of the cupboard and staring at Ferguson.

"Your poem," Ferguson said, pointing again. "I was just about to read it."

But even as Ferguson spoke, his grandfather charged across the room and yanked the poem off the wall, tacks flying in every direction.

"It's not that good," his grandfather declared.

"Why was Laverne in your poem?" Ferguson asked.

He had managed to read her name before the

poem was snatched away. "And the word 'yearn'?" he added.

"Not much rhymes with Laverne," his grandfather muttered.

Ferguson studied his grandfather. Were his cheeks getting red?

"Here's the paint," his grandfather said, returning to the cupboard and thrusting several pots Ferguson's way without making eye contact.

They worked on the life ring in awkward silence, while Ferguson wondered what was going on.

"That looks good," his grandfather observed when they had finished the job, but still not looking Ferguson in the eye.

"This will be a nice addition to the show," Ferguson confirmed.

"So you'll bring your ping-pong paddle tomorrow?" his grandfather reminded him.

"You bet," Ferguson said, deciding it was best not to mention the poem again.

On Monday after school, Ferguson went to retrieve his favorite paddle, hidden on top of his bedroom bookshelves.

It was missing.

Ferguson stormed to the dining room where the table continued to be covered with a dozen school projects in various stages of completion. It was here that he had often located missing items built into half-baked homework assignments, with no one (no one!) ever asking his permission to borrow his things.

He scanned the table: a measuring scale, a catapult, green stuff growing in various clay pots, a color wheel, stacks of petri dishes, a disassembled calculator, an ant farm, an album of pressed seaweed, a paper pinhole camera, circuit boards, a model of the solar system and a diorama of a snowy scene with a frozen pond, complete with Plasticine skaters.

Wait a minute! The frozen pond looked suspiciously like his ping-pong paddle wrapped in tinfoil.

Ferguson tossed the skaters headfirst into the Plasticine snowbank, unwrapped his paddle and headed out to Sunset Manor. He rounded the corner and passed below Graeme's house when he heard his name.

Ferguson stopped to look up. He smiled when he saw that it was Graeme, bounding down his front steps.

But then someone else standing beside Fetch on Graeme's porch caught his attention.

"Where are you headed?" Graeme asked as the two set off together.

"I'm going to play ping-pong with my granddad," Ferguson said. He patted the paddle that was tucked into his back pocket. "Is that *Norris* on your porch?"

Both boys looked back at Graeme's house.

Norris ducked behind the cover of a lilac bush by the porch, a beat too late.

"Yes. That's Norris," Graeme admitted. He kept walking.

"I'm dying to know why you're hanging around with *him*," Ferguson pressed while Graeme matched his steady stride. "You're not the type who likes cheaters."

"He cheats?" Graeme asked.

"Constantly," Ferguson said. "He's always trying to copy my answers during spelling tests. I tell him to stop, but, like my granddad says, I might as well flog a dead horse. Norris makes me mad enough to spit feathers!"

"Geez Louise," Graeme said sympathetically.

They walked without comment, while Ferguson

whistled a tune he had picked up from the many funeral services he had attended.

"I wonder why Ms. Penfield put him in charge of her plants," Graeme pondered out loud.

"Heaven knows," Ferguson said, shrugging. "Here's my turn," he added, pointing up a small street that intersected the main one they were on.

"I'll keep you company," Graeme offered, and he made the turn with Ferguson.

They walked for a few more blocks while Ferguson practiced his whistling.

"Those plants," Graeme continued between songs. "They can't be safe with Norris."

"Ms. Penfield was dead wrong to trust him," Ferguson agreed. "Plus, like I said, he cheats."

Ferguson came to a halt. "Well, here I am."

Ferguson and Graeme stood to survey Sunset Manor: the green lawn sporting careful flowerbeds; outdoor furniture arranged in various groupings; old people moving with canes and

walkers; and, remarkably, someone flying a
bat-shaped kite that made swooping passes at
everyone below.

"Your grandfather lives *here*?" Graeme asked.

"That's him with the kite," Ferguson said,
pointing proudly.

The kite flyer waved.

"How often do you visit him?" Graeme asked.

"Every day," Ferguson said.

"Interesting," Graeme said.

Ferguson's grandfather slowly started to walk
toward them, tugging the sky-high bat along.
The boys watched the kite's every move. But
the next question that Graeme asked was not
about the kite.

Foghorn

Ferguson's grandfather took a few steps closer to the boys, then paused to allow the kite to recover from yet another nosedive.

"Did you miss any days this past week?" Graeme asked about Ferguson's visits to Sunset Manor.

Ferguson turned to him, puzzled. Graeme had never taken such a detailed interest in him before.

"No. I always come here straight from school. If it's not ping-pong, then it's Scrabble, or crafts or maybe some outing. Look, there's

Mr. Hastings, my granddad's friend. He must have come back from his ear appointment already."

Tupper Hastings nodded at Ferguson from his lawn chair, then ducked from the suicidal kite.

"Ear appointment?" Graeme repeated.

"Mr. Hastings is deaf as a doornail," Ferguson explained. "But that doesn't stop him from talking on and on about the boat he used to own. Old fishing stories never die."

"Do you know what the name of his boat was?" Graeme asked.

"Yes," Ferguson said, but he could not completely recall the name of Tupper Hastings's boat. "*Something Dawn.*"

He was about to pull out his notepad to check, but Graeme interrupted.

"*Crack of Dawn?*" Graeme offered.

"That's it! *Crack of Dawn*," Ferguson said.

"And your grandfather," Graeme continued. "You say he's friends with Mr. Hastings?"

"They were both fishermen," Ferguson confirmed.

"So your grandfather owned a boat, too?"

"Yes. *Fog Burner.*" Ferguson shaded his eyes to better view the bat with the death wish.

His grandfather had almost worked his way to within earshot, kite still swooping manically against the mackerel sky.

"Here he comes now," Ferguson said, enjoying Graeme's interest. "Do you want to meet him?"

But Graeme said, "Another time," and hurried away.

Must be going to feed the giant lobster, Ferguson reasoned.

"Who was that?" Ferguson's grandfather asked.

"Graeme," said Ferguson. "His dad was the

fisherman who caught the giant lobster. Graeme's been feeding it at the community museum."

"Are we still going Wednesday to see it at lunch? I can't face those geezly fish cakes, remember?"

"You bet," Ferguson said.

"Heads up!" Ferguson's grandfather shouted just before the bat kite dive-bombed Laverne Bridge, who had unfortunately stepped onto the lawn for a game of croquet.

The next day, during his visit with his grandfather, Ferguson reported on the stranger he had seen on his way to Sunset Manor. She had been standing on the government wharf as he passed by.

"I think she was a journalist," he said to his grandfather.

Ferguson was not surprised to see a journalist in Lower Narrow Spit. After all, he found the stories of his community fascinating. That was why he recorded them in such detail.

"She held out a microphone," Ferguson continued, "and it looked as if she was interviewing Graeme and his dad."

"About the giant lobster?" his grandfather deduced.

"Must be," Ferguson said. "And then I saw something really funny. Mr. Fowler stormed out of the cannery and headed straight down the wharf. It looked as if he was trying to interrupt them."

"Sounds like Fowler," his grandfather said. "Has to be the center of everything. You'd think that owning the town's only cannery would be enough."

Ferguson nodded. He had once peeked into Mr. Fowler's office after dropping off a lunch to Iris, who had forgotten it at home. He had been delighted to spy Norris's paperweight, now completely dried out, on Mr. Fowler's desk.

The little boat inside looked as if it had been shipwrecked. But when he had pulled back, he was horrified to discover that the office walls were covered in hunting trophies featuring heads of a grizzly bear, an Alaska wolf, an antelope, a mule deer, two elk, a bighorn sheep, a bull moose and a buffalo.

It had given Ferguson nightmares for weeks.

"We'll pick you and Mr. Hastings up at noon tomorrow," Ferguson reminded his grandfather as he got up to leave.

The next day, Ferguson's mom dropped him off at the community museum, along with his grandfather, Tupper Hastings and three lunch bags.

"Be good, boys," she quipped as they piled out of the van, the words "Forever and For Always" painted in giant flowery letters on both sides. "I'll pick you up in forty-five minutes so that Ferguson can get back in time for his afternoon classes."

Ferguson led the way through the double doors of the old train station into the main exhibit.

"We're here!" his grandfather shouted to Tupper Hastings.

"What?" Tupper Hastings said.

Ferguson paused so that they could get their bearings. A class of grade fours visiting from a nearby county surrounded the tank housing the giant lobster. And off to the side, in the cannery display area of the museum, Ferguson spotted Graeme, who was studying the lobster-claw plaque that the McDermits had donated.

"Hi, Graeme!" Ferguson called out, remembering Graeme's friendliness during their recent walk to Sunset Manor. "My granddad and Mr. Hastings are here to see your giant lobster!"

"Great," Graeme said, looking their way briefly, then returning his attention to the plaque.

"There it is, dead ahead," Ferguson said to his

grandfather and Tupper Hastings as he pointed to the tank.

"What?" Tupper Hastings said, adjusting his hearing aid.

Ferguson led them over to the mega lobster. The grade four class divided to let the seniors and Ferguson through.

"What's this?" Ferguson's grandfather asked.

He had spied an old newspaper article posted on the wall near the tank.

The caption read "Giant Lobster Captured!" The year was 1977.

Ferguson and his grandfather peered at the grainy black-and-white photograph in the yellowed article. McDermit was crouched beside a mammoth crustacean. Lobster boats were tied up along both sides of the wharf.

"Hey, Granddad! This was the article that McDermit showed me in his scrapbook. See, here's your boat, *Fog Burner*!" Ferguson said, pointing to the photograph. "Mr. Hastings, here's your boat, too!"

"What?" Tupper Hastings said.

The grade four teacher walked over to Ferguson's grandfather and asked a question.

"We noticed that the lobster in the photograph and the lobster in this tank are both left-handed. But giant lobsters are rare. So we were wondering if this lobster might be the same one as the lobster in that old photograph."

The children watched Ferguson's grandfather with eager eyes.

"So! You all know that lobsters can be left- or right-handed by which side their crusher claw is on," Ferguson's grandfather confirmed with the grade fours, his gravelly voice softening at the edges.

Heads bobbed.

"Maybe you could tell us more about this story," said the teacher to Ferguson's grandfather while pointing to the article.

"If it's yarns you want from a couple of retired old fishermen," Ferguson's grandfather said, throwing his arm around Tupper Hastings's shoulders, "then we've got plenty to tell."

"What?" Tupper Hastings said.

Ferguson's grandfather turned to Ferguson. "Why don't you call your friend over?"

Ferguson stepped out from the crowd.

"Hey, Graeme! Come on over," he called. "My granddad wants to tell you something."

"Sure thing," Graeme called back.

He made his way to the group.

"Your lobster's in awful good shape," Ferguson's grandfather remarked.

"What?" Tupper Hastings said.

"Thanks," Graeme said, shoving his hands into his pockets.

"I was on the wharf when McDermit caught his lobster," Ferguson's grandfather said, pointing his knurly finger at the posted article.

By then, Ms. Carrington had joined the crowd. She spoke.

"I was wondering. McDermit never donated a mounted giant lobster to the museum. Do you know if he set it free?"

In the distance, a foghorn sounded.

"No, he didn't," Ferguson's grandfather said matter-of-factly.

Everyone waited for more.

"What happened to it?" she finally asked.

"McDermit's lobster died," Ferguson's grandfather explained. "Something about the change in water temperature or the salt level in the brine. I can't quite recall."

"It died?" Graeme repeated.

"It was McDermit's biggest regret," Ferguson's grandfather continued. "McDermit told us that something surviving that long should have been returned to the sea."

The heads in the crowd started to nod, one by one.

Ferguson studied his grandfather standing next to the ancient lobster. He was struck with just how much his grandfather still missed McDermit. His memories were still fresh, even raw, like the sea he had spent his life on. After all this time, his grandfather could still remember McDermit's exact words.

And his regrets.

Ferguson nodded gravely along with the rest.

"What?" Tupper Hastings said.

Trophy

"Hey, you're getting better!" Ferguson declared during Thursday's visit as he watched his grandfather cut across the lawn in an attempt to control the wildly dipping bat kite.

The rest of the residents were inside, observing safely from behind the window of the recreation room.

In truth, his grandfather looked as if he was ready to give up. Ferguson soon learned the reason. When the kite spitefully drove itself into the ground for a dead stop, Ferguson's grandfather turned to him and said, "I can't stop thinking about that giant lobster."

Upon hearing those words, Ferguson deeply regretted his earlier promise to take Sunset Manor residents to the lobster supper and auction. And yet, there was nothing else to do that evening because the entire town would be attending the big event, making it impossible for Ferguson to come up with an alternative plan.

On Friday, just before the lobster festival weekend, Ferguson could feel eyes boring into him as he sat at his desk. He knew who it was without even looking.

Norris.

Ferguson instinctively hunkered down over his spelling test, annoyed that Ms. Penfield's fill-in teacher had stepped out of the classroom to speak with the principal in the hall, leaving Ferguson to defend himself.

"I'm not cheating," Norris whispered. "I've got something to tell you."

"Go away," Ferguson said, swatting at the air in Norris's general direction.

"Ms. Penfield's orange-flowered cactus is missing," Norris whispered.

Ferguson looked over at their teacher's crowded plant collection in the window. The one with the orange flower was not there.

"I knew it! She was crazy putting you in charge."

"Graeme thought you might have had something to do with it," Norris whispered.

"What?!" Ferguson said loudly, sitting bolt upright.

"Shhhhh!" others whispered from all around.

Ferguson turned to Graeme, who was sitting a few rows away.

Graeme had been watching their exchange but quickly looked down at his own work and refused to return Ferguson's questioning stare.

Could it be true? Up until now, Ferguson had considered Graeme a friend. Then again, he had not been all that sociable at Sunset Manor when Ferguson had tried to introduce Graeme to his grandfather. And Graeme had not been happy at the museum when Ferguson's grandfather told everyone that he thought the giant lobster should be released.

But still. Why would Graeme think Ferguson had done something nasty to Ms. Penfield's cactus?

"Graeme's been investigating for me," Norris whispered. "He thinks it could have been Georgia or Deckland, too."

Georgia and Deckland now turned their heads in Norris's direction.

Investigating? What was Norris talking about? Ferguson's mouth went dry.

"Tests forward, please," their fill-in teacher demanded upon returning to the classroom.

Ferguson sat, unable to move, while papers flew around and past him.

"Is that why he walked with me the other day to Sunset Manor?" Ferguson asked in a small voice.

The bell rang.

"Some people's kids," Norris said brightly, getting up from his desk.

Ferguson sat numbly. But as his mind cleared, he began to focus on Graeme.

How dare he suspect Ferguson!

Ferguson stood to confront him. But Graeme had already made a narrow escape, and no matter where Ferguson looked at recess, he could not find his accuser.

Ferguson pushed his fuming thoughts aside when he arrived at Sunset Manor so that he could help his grandfather put the final touches on the Know the Ropes Show. One look at the tables already crowded with artifacts told Ferguson that the exhibit had all the makings of a legacy. He was also certain that the event would get his grandfather's mind off the giant lobster.

"Good job," Buddy Clark said, thumping Ferguson's grandfather on the back as retired fishermen began to fill the common room.

Ferguson was hanging his grandfather's life ring when he spotted Tupper Hastings approaching Norris at the front door. Ferguson joined them.

"I see you made it," Ferguson said. "This is Mr. Hastings."

"Nice to meet you," Norris said, clutching his knapsack and taking everything in.

"This is called the common room," Ferguson explained. "We had to move the furniture to make space for the exhibit."

Norris and Ferguson worked their way over to the display after helping themselves to glasses of purple-colored punch.

"Here we are," Ferguson said with a grand sweep of his hand.

Norris looked up and down the exhibit, which featured fishing gear, boat tools of every description, captains' wheels and nameplates mounted on the walls, including *Fog Burner* and *Crack of Dawn*.

Ferguson's grandfather joined them, all smiles.

"And this is my granddad," Ferguson said, swinging his arm around his grandfather's shoulders.

"Nice to meet you," Ferguson's grandfather said, shaking Norris's hand.

"So what did you bring of McDermit's?" Ferguson asked.

Norris pulled out a framed shed-door handle from his knapsack and handed it to Ferguson.

"It's a homemade door handle," Ferguson observed.

His grandfather leaned in for a better look at the intricate carving.

"Looks like McDermit's handiwork all right," he acknowledged.

"It's from McDermit's fish shed," Norris confirmed.

"You took it right off the door?" Ferguson asked, alarm creeping into his voice.

"No," Norris said dismissively. "The shed was torn down when we added our tennis court at Marshy Hope. This is all that's left."

"McDermit's fish shed is gone?" Ferguson's grandfather asked, rubbing his stubbled chin with his large, knurly fingers.

"Sure," Norris said matter-of-factly. "It was old and useless and in the way."

Ferguson was stunned. How could Norris be so callous?

Ferguson glanced apologetically at his grandfather, hoping that he might let that cruel remark go.

Ferguson's grandfather cleared his throat.

"I think I'll go get myself some punch," he said quietly.

But he did not go to the punch bowl. Instead, he lowered himself onto one of the couches that was pushed into a corner at the far end of the room and stared at nothing at all.

Ferguson thrust the framed door handle back to Norris.

"Why'd you go and say that?" Ferguson demanded.

"What?" Norris asked, all innocent.

"Getting rid of things that are *old* and *useless* and *in the way*?!" Ferguson said, imitating Norris's weasel voice. "You really know how to cheer folks up around here!"

Although Norris's ears went pink, he gave Ferguson a curt wave of his hand and said, "I can fix it."

He proceeded to stand on the seat of a nearby chair.

"Can I please have everybody's attention?"

The din quieted, and the exhibit-goers turned politely to face Norris.

"As you probably all know, a giant lobster has been caught in our bay and will be auctioned off during tomorrow's annual lobster festival."

Oh, no, thought Ferguson. He did not want his grandfather to be reminded of anybody's giant lobster.

"Well, what if there are bidders from all over? That lobster could end up almost anywhere! But my dad thinks that it should stay in Lower Narrow Spit, and he's going to see to that. He promises to be the highest bidder and turn it into a trophy for our community's biggest building: the Lucky Catch Cannery!"

Norris beamed, hands on hips.

Then he looked around.

Norris, to his bewilderment, was surrounded by stunned silence.

Jaws dropped.

Nobody spoke, including Ferguson. Instead, his grandfather's words about McDermit's biggest regret replayed over and over in his head.

Ferguson's grandfather slowly rose to his feet.

"McDermit caught a lobster like that in his day. And I was on the wharf when he hauled it in."

"I know. But it didn't end up as a trophy. Now we'll have one. Right here. In Lower Narrow Spit," Norris said, stopping and starting while looking to the crowd for support.

"There's no trophy because McDermit's lobster died," Ferguson's grandfather said gravely. "It was McDermit's biggest regret. McDermit told us that something that old should have been returned to the sea."

Ferguson's grandfather fixed Norris with a stony look, then sank back down.

Accusing stares from around the room bored into Norris.

Norris scrambled off the chair. He looked desperately around for Ferguson.

But Ferguson wanted nothing more to do with Norris. He stood holding the front door wide open for the unwelcome guest.

Lucky Catch

Taking down the Know the Ropes Show had been a very glum affair. Everyone, including Buddy Clark, Heimlich Fester and even Laverne Bridge set about their tasks quietly, while Ferguson fumed about Norris and Graeme in equal measure.

He knew that he was back to square one with his grandfather's legacy problem. Worse still, his grandfather was tormented by the giant lobster.

"It should be set free," he kept muttering to himself, big hands crossed helplessly on his lap.

The only thing Ferguson could think of to do

was set aside his anger with Graeme and convince him to forget about the auction and release the spectacular catch.

With grim determination, Ferguson marched to the museum that Saturday, which was also the day of the lobster festival. He was certain he would run into Graeme, who would be feeding the prized lobster one last time before it was moved to the old dance hall where the auction would be held that evening.

The museum was crowded with festival participants, but Graeme was not among them.

"You just missed him," Ms. Carrington explained, busy setting up for the lobster chowder contest. "But he told me that he's quite excited about tonight's auction. There's sure to be a bidding war!"

"What do you mean?" Ferguson asked, thinking that Norris's father was the only one in Lower Narrow Spit with enough money to bid.

"A marine biologist from Big Fish Aquarium arrived in town this morning, and he wants to buy the lobster for their tank on northern waters."

Ferguson frowned. He knew what a bidding war meant. There would be no way that Graeme could be talked into releasing the giant lobster now.

Unless.

Unless Ferguson's grandfather could somehow win the lobster and then release it!

"See you at the auction!" Ms. Carrington called as Ferguson dashed out the doors and onto Main Street, which was thick with festival supporters.

Ferguson completely ignored the parade that was passing and flew by the lobster trap competition on the government wharf as he made a beeline to Sunset Manor. His grandfather was napping outside on a lawn chair. Heimlich Fester sat beside him, peering suspiciously at the sky with his binoculars.

"Granddad," Ferguson said, gently shaking his grandfather's shoulder.

His grandfather opened his eyes one at a time.

"*We're* going to bid on the giant lobster!"

"We don't have that kind of money," his grandfather said, still groggy from having been woken up.

"But if we ask your friends to help, if we pool our money, we could win! And then we could set the giant lobster free! Wouldn't that be an incredible legacy?"

Ferguson studied his grandfather's face as his grandfather worked out Ferguson's idea. Others around them soon caught on.

"I'm in," announced Buddy Clark from his nearby chair.

"Me, too," Laverne Bridge said, her brooch glinting in the sun.

Heimlich Fester set down his binoculars and also nodded.

"What?" Tupper Hastings said, adjusting his hearing aid.

Ferguson's grandfather slapped the arms of his chair with glee.

After that night's sold-out lobster supper of boiled lobsters, potato salad and blueberry buckle, everyone rushed to the chairs that had been lined up in the old dance hall for the auction. Ferguson and the residents from Sunset Manor took up a whole row near the back so they could see everything that was going on.

Graeme had managed to grab three seats that were only a few rows from the front podium. His dad sat on one side; a man wearing a staff shirt with the Big Fish Aquarium logo sat on the other. In the center of the front row sat Norris and Norris's dad. Behind them, Allen fired spitballs at the back of Norris's head, with Georgia and Deckland egging him on from the sidelines. Nearby sat Ferguson's sisters, gushing over Ms. Penfield and her brand-new baby girl.

"Did you hear what happened to Ms. Penfield's cactus?" Georgia had asked Ferguson, just before he took his seat.

"I know *I* didn't have anything to do with it," Ferguson replied, getting mad all over again.

"Of course you didn't. Me either. It was Norris all along. He accidentally broke the flower off, then hid the plant in the compost."

"Ms. Penfield must be mad," Ferguson said.

"No," Georgia said. "I overheard him tell her what really happened, and she said that he was brave to confess!"

"Norris," Ferguson said bitterly. "I could just spit feathers."

As Ferguson sat down, he glowered at both Norris and Graeme, unwilling to forgive either of his classmates quite so quickly.

On stage, various items to be auctioned off were displayed: a free membership to the curling rink; a crate of canned lobster packed on ice; knitted fisherman's sweaters; a gift basket from the drugstore; a voucher for lunch for two at the Chinese restaurant; gardening tools; homemade pies; crafts made by residents at Sunset Manor; and one monster lobster staring out from its tank.

The town's postmaster, who also volunteered as the auctioneer, stepped up to the podium. The town's mayor stood behind him to assist with the bidding.

A hush filled the room. Several reporters and camera operators positioned themselves along the aisle, recording the whole event. Ferguson settled confidently in his chair.

"Good evening and welcome," the auctioneer boomed. "Let's waste no time and get straight to the bidding. First up, a crate of the finest canned lobster in the world, generously donated by Lower Narrow Spit's very own cannery."

"That's Lucky Catch," Norris's dad added. He half stood and waved to the crowd.

"Now, who wants to start the opening bid?" the auctioneer asked jovially.

Ferguson leaned over to his grandfather. "When will the giant lobster be auctioned?" he asked.

"Probably after everything else has been sold. Think you'll be able to stand the suspense?"

Ferguson nodded eagerly. He was in no hurry. This was going to be great!

"Hey, bada-bada-bada," the auctioneer called as bids started to roll in.

The auction went on and on, one item selling after another. Slowly, slowly the stage grew bare. And then, at long last, only the giant lobster remained.

Ferguson was giddy with anticipation.

"Well, ladies and gentlemen. That concludes

Lower Narrow Spit's annual lobster auction. We've got nothing left to sell ... no, wait. What's this?" the auctioneer joked, turning to the giant crustacean in mock amazement.

The crowd laughed at his antics.

Ferguson's grandfather playfully elbowed Ferguson in the ribs.

"Do I have an opening bid?" the auctioneer asked.

Mr. Fowler arrogantly held up his paddle and waved to the cameras.

"Hey, bada-bada-bada," the auctioneer droned. "Hey, bada-bada-bada."

Ferguson turned his gaze to Graeme's little group, certain of what would happen next.

Sure enough, the marine biologist put up his paddle, too.

"We have a second bidder!" the auctioneer announced with surprise.

Both Norris and his dad wheeled around to see who would dare outbid them.

"Hey, bada-bada-bada," the auctioneer called. "Hey, bada-bada-bada."

Mr. Fowler rammed his paddle into the air.

"Hey, bada-bada-bada. Hey, bada-bada-bada."

The marine biologist shot his paddle up in retaliation.

"Hey, bada-bada-bada. Hey, bada-bada-bada."

Back and forth. Back and forth. The bids getting higher and higher. The back of Mr. Fowler's neck turning the color of boiled lobster.

Then he shouted to the auctioneer. "Let's put an end to this silliness! I'll give you *double* what the last bidder gave!"

The crowd gasped, and there was a flurry of whispering between Graeme and the marine biologist.

The marine biologist hesitated, then signaled

to the auctioneer that he was still in the game. But Ferguson noticed that his paddle was shaking.

The crowd leaned forward in their seats. All eyes turned to Norris's dad.

Mr. Fowler sat staring straight ahead. Norris looked up at his dad, then back at the stranger bidding against them, then to his dad again.

Nobody breathed.

Ferguson watched in amused fascination.

"Hey, bada-bada-bada. Hey, bada-bada-bada."

Norris's dad slowly raised his paddle, electrifying the crowd.

The crowd shifted in their seats, then turned to the marine biologist with great expectations.

But the marine biologist slumped his shoulders and laid his paddle on his lap. Outbid, Graeme put his head in his hands.

"Ready?" Ferguson's grandfather whispered.

"You bet," Ferguson replied, barely able to keep seated.

Ferguson's grandfather stood.

"Now hold your horses!" he called out. "That lobster's not sold yet! It's our turn to join the bidding!"

Legacy

Ferguson beamed. His grandfather clutched a paddle in his big-knuckled fist and thrust it into the air. The reporters and camera operators adjusted their equipment to record the thrilling turn of events.

"Something that's survived so long deserves to be set free," Ferguson's grandfather declared, speaking directly to the cameras. "That's what McDermit always told us."

"So we've pooled our money, and we're going to bid in his memory!" Ferguson added, waving a wad of money in the air as proof.

The audience buzzed with approval.

The auctioneer started up again with renewed vigor.

"Hey, bada-bada-bada. Hey, bada-bada-bada."

Mr. Fowler kept his back to the audience when he raised his paddle and nodded deliberately at the auctioneer.

The audience muttered unhappily.

"Hey, bada-bada-bada. Hey, bada-bada-bada."

Ferguson's grandfather jabbed the air with his paddle.

The audience whooped and stomped their feet.

"Hey, bada-bada-bada. Hey, bada-bada-bada."

Mr. Fowler responded with his paddle held up for all to see.

The audience made grumpy noises.

"Hey, bada-bada-bada. Hey, bada-bada-bada," the auctioneer said, tugging at his collar.

Oh, no, thought Ferguson. The bidding had

already reached the amount of money that Sunset Manor had collected!

Ferguson's grandfather motioned for the seniors to gather in a huddle, along with Ferguson.

"Try one more bid," Buddy Clark urged.

"Are you sure?" Ferguson's grandfather asked.

"I've got you covered," said the retired cowboy, patting his wallet. "Just try once more," he urged.

The huddle cleared, and Ferguson's grandfather raised his paddle again. But Ferguson knew, along with the entire audience, that this was the absolutely last bid they could manage.

Mr. Fowler studied the situation. Then he turned back to the auctioneer with a grin and jingled the coins in his pocket with his free hand. He raised his paddle one last time with the confidence of the owner of the town's only cannery.

"Hey, bada-bada-bada," the auctioneer said, mustering no enthusiasm whatsoever.

Ferguson swallowed hard, as if he had

been whacked in the head by one of Norris's dodgeballs.

Ferguson's grandfather shook his empty fist in the air, muttered a blue curse, then sat down. His buddies reached over from their chairs to thump his back in sympathy. Ferguson gave him a hug.

"Sold to the highest bidder," the auctioneer announced flatly. "I'm sure this giant lobster will make a fine trophy for the cannery, to be enjoyed by the folks of Lower Narrow Spit for years and years to come."

Ferguson sat down. He tasted something bad in his mouth.

"I won!" Norris's dad exclaimed.

A smidgen of applause flittered across the room.

Mr. Fowler stood and cleared his throat. He began making his way to the podium to say a few words, having paid a princely sum for his trophy.

And then something totally unexpected happened.

Norris bolted from his chair and scooted past his dad to the podium. He quickly bent the microphone down to his height.

"I want everyone to know," Norris announced, rushing his words, "that my dad has decided to set the giant lobster free!"

Mr. Fowler froze in mid-stride. He sputtered, and his mouth stuck half open. It was clear that he had promised nothing of the sort.

Ferguson looked at Norris in disbelief. And then Graeme chimed in.

"Hear, hear!" Graeme exclaimed to the stunned audience. He jumped to his feet and began to clap.

From across the room, Ferguson hesitated briefly, a beat behind Graeme. But when he realized that his grandfather had somehow gotten his wish without the winning bid, Ferguson stood and clapped, too. The audience roared their applause and joined the standing ovation.

Mr. Fowler turned to the audience. His furious look gave way to surprise, then to a flattered smile. Norris stepped away from the microphone to make room for his dad at the podium. Mr. Fowler grabbed Norris's hand, and the two faced the cheering crowd, arms held up in victory.

Ferguson and his grandfather did the same.

The crowd went wild.

The next morning arrived well before sunrise at Sunset Manor. After the auction, Graeme's dad had invited Ferguson, his grandfather, Tupper Hastings, the marine biologist and the Fowlers on an early morning expedition to set the giant lobster free. So Ferguson had slept overnight on his grandfather's guest cot.

Ferguson and his grandfather entered the dark and empty cafeteria.

"Hungry?" Ferguson's grandfather asked loudly, sending the silence scurrying in all directions.

"You bet," Ferguson said, still rubbing his eyes.

He had never been up at this hour, and his thoughts were foggy.

Not so for Ferguson's grandfather. He busied himself in the kitchen, banging cupboard doors, rattling cutlery and humming a sea shanty, as if he had been up for hours.

Ferguson sat at a nearby table and watched him in amazement. Tupper Hastings soon joined Ferguson, a big grin on his face.

"Top of the morning!" Ferguson's grandfather called out when he noticed that Tupper Hastings had arrived.

"What?" Tupper Hastings said.

Ferguson's grandfather hustled over with plates of bacon and tomato sandwiches on burnt toast.

Ferguson had never seen him move so fast, so effortlessly. He and Tupper Hastings gobbled up their breakfasts in lickety-split time, chatting all the while about former fishing days.

They were so busy exchanging stories that they did not see Ferguson's mom enter the room. Ferguson waved her over.

"Good morning, Dad," she said, holding her van keys in one hand and bending down to kiss Ferguson's grandfather on the cheek. "Ready to go? You don't want to miss the boat."

Chairs scraped against the floor, and everyone made for the van. The words "Forever and For Always," written on its sides, glowed in the rising sunlight. They were the first to arrive at the wharf.

"I was thinking about all the things I liked when I used to get up this early," Ferguson's grandfather said as they tumbled out of the van.

"The way the dewy grass squeaked under your rubber boots," Ferguson's mom said. "The weight of your metal lunch bucket with homemade rolls inside. The bounce of *Fog Burner* when you jumped aboard."

"Pulling up the first trap before sunrise and finding more than one lobster inside. The smell of the tropics after a hurricane blew through. The clanging of the channel buoy as you motored by," Ferguson added after consulting his notepad.

Ferguson's grandfather stared at his daughter and then his grandson.

He blinked.

"What?" Tupper Hastings said, reaching for Ferguson's notepad. He flipped through pages and pages filled with Sunset Manor stories, and as he did, his weathered face softened. He handed the notepad back to Ferguson, thumped Ferguson's grandfather on the back, and then he and Ferguson's mom strolled down to the end of the wharf to look out at the sea.

"It's a great day to set a giant lobster free," Ferguson declared.

"Sure, sure," Ferguson's grandfather replied.

"But releasing a giant lobster isn't going to be my legacy."

Ferguson could not believe it. His grandfather was impossible! Crestfallen, he staggered backward, nearly falling off the wharf into the water, but dropping his notepad so that its pages splayed against the damp wood planks.

"What's a better legacy than a legendary giant lobster?!" Ferguson demanded, ignoring his sopping notes.

His grandfather took in a deep breath of the salty morning air and released it slowly. He wore the gargantuan smile of a proud old fisherman as he bent down to retrieve Ferguson's notepad and carefully wipe its covers on his pants.

"My grandson," his grandfather replied. He handed the notepad back to Ferguson. "And now it's time to write some new stories," he added. "You might want to start with characters your own age."

Ferguson heard the crunch of gravel. There was a sweep of headlights, then the sound of car doors slamming from the parking lot of the cannery. The others had started to arrive.

"Norris and Graeme," Ferguson said.

He opened his notepad to a fresh page.

Acknowledgments

In an oddly comforting way, this last book in my lobster trilogy was inspired by my dad. I never really knew him while I grew up on the Canadian prairies, because he spent so much of the time running his business, or rather, keeping his business afloat. He died of a terminal illness when I was in my early twenties, but not before coming out with my mom to visit us in Nova Scotia and to marvel at the ocean. He was especially fascinated by the tides and by the local lobster fishermen, whom he watched hauling traps from our living room window. He was impressed that they worked even in blizzards to make each day of their short lobster season count. He was, however, openly squeamish about cooking live lobster. Despite the fancy cowboy boots he insisted on wearing, he had, as I had always suspected, a soft side.

My mom reported that one of the last comments he made to her as he lay dying in hospital was that he was proud of his two daughters.

And so, I wrote the last lines of this trilogy with him in mind.

That, and Buddy Clark's cowboy boots.